Praise for The Imaginatio

These books are a great combination of history and adventure in a clean manner perfect for young children.

—Margie B., *My Springfield Mommy* blog

These books will help my kids enjoy history.

—Beth S., third-grade public school teacher
Colorado Springs, Colorado

[The Imagination Station books] focus on God much more than the Magic Tree House books do.

—Emilee, age 7, Waynesboro, Pennsylvania

My nine-year-old son has already read [the first two books], one of them twice. He is very eager to read more in the series too. I am planning on reading them out loud to my younger son.

—Abbi C., mother of four, Minnesota

FOCUS ON THE FAMILY® PRESENTS
THE IMAGINATION STATION®

Problems in Plymouth

BOOK 6

**MARIANNE HERING • MARSHAL YOUNGER
CREATIVE DIRECTOR: PAUL McCUSKER
ILLUSTRATED BY DAVID HOHN**

TYNDALE

FOCUS ON THE FAMILY • ADVENTURES IN ODYSSEY
TYNDALE HOUSE PUBLISHERS, INC. • CAROL STREAM, ILLINOIS

ISBN: 978-1-58997-632-0 (alk. paper)

A Focus on the Family book published by Tyndale House Publishers, Inc., Carol Stream, Illinois 60188

Cover design by Michael Heath | Magnus Creative

Library of Congress Cataloging-in-Publication Data
Hering, Marianne.
Problems in Plymouth / Marianne Hering, Marshal Younger ; illustrated by David Hohn.
    p. cm. -- (The Imagination Station ; bk. 6)
"Focus on the Family."
Summary: When time-traveling cousins Patrick and Beth use the Imagination Station to go to Plymouth Colony in 1621 hoping to find Hugh and return him to his own time, they meet William Bradford, Myles Standish, and Squanto.
[1. Space and time--Fiction. 2. Pilgrims (New Plymouth Colony)--Fiction. 3. Nauset Indians--Fiction. 4. Wampanoag Indians--Fiction. 5. Indians of North America--Massachusetts--Fiction. 6. Cousins--Fiction. 7. Christian life--Fiction. 8. Plymouth (Mass.)--History--17th century--Fiction.] I. Younger, Marshal. II. Hohn, David, 1974- ill. III. Title.
    PZ7.H431258Pro 2011
    [Fic]--dc23   2011033313

Printed in the United States of America
5 6 7 8 9 / 16 15 14 13

For manufacturing information regarding this product, please call 1-800-323-9400.

To Cory,

The day you first came through our door, I had no idea how many train books we would read or how many injuries we would incur in our wrestling matches, or how many pretend guys we would vanquish together or how proud I would be to have this conversation for the rest of my life:

"Are you Cory's dad?"

"Yes. Yes I am." —MY

Contents

Prologue

This story begins with an older gentleman named Mr. Whittaker. He's an inventor who owns a shop called Whit's End.

Mr. Whittaker built the Imagination Station. It lets kids see history in person. It's a lot like a time machine.

One day two cousins, Patrick and Beth, came to Whit's End. They wanted to use the Imagination Station. But Mr. Whittaker said it had stopped working.

Patrick and Beth were disappointed. Then Patrick touched the Imagination Station. Suddenly the machine lit up!

Mr. Whittaker was surprised. He told the cousins about his last trip in the Imagination Station. He had visited a relative named Albert, who lived in England long ago.

The men gave each other special rings. Albert gave Mr. Whittaker a ring with a rose on it. Mr. Whittaker gave Albert a ring with a knight's head on it—the Whittaker crest.

Then Albert got in trouble. He was accused of stealing treasures from Lord Darkthorn, his master. Mr. Whittaker found notes in the Imagination Station. The notes asked him to help Albert replace the missing treasures.

The cousins went on four adventures to help Albert. They visited the Vikings, the ancient Romans, Kublai Khan, and an English castle.

In England, an evil man named Hugh took the ring that Mr. Whittaker had given Albert. It seemed to summon the Imagination Station. Hugh jumped into the machine and disappeared in time.

The cousins followed him to ancient Israel. Patrick and Beth helped stop Hugh from changing the David and Goliath story. The cousins got back the special ring. But Hugh escaped into time again.

Now Patrick and Beth are starting a new

adventure. They must follow Hugh and stop him from causing problems in history. Then they must get Hugh back to his own time.

Can the cousins do it?

The New Mission

Mr. Whittaker's eyes were fixed on the Imagination Station. He tapped a finger against his chin. He frowned. Then he placed his hands on the keyboard.

Beth and Patrick watched. For ten minutes Mr. Whittaker had been using the Imagination Station's computer to track Hugh somewhere in time.

Finally Mr. Whittaker smiled. "I found him," he said.

Beth and Patrick stepped closer.

"Where is he?" Patrick asked.

He pointed to the computer screen.

"Sixteen twenty-one," Mr. Whittaker said.

"Is that an address or a year?" Beth asked.

"A year," said Mr. Whittaker. "The address is the Plymouth Colony."

Beth recognized the name. "That's where the Pilgrims landed in America!"

she said.

Mr. Whittaker nodded.

Patrick said, "They came on a ship called the *Mayflower*, right?"

Mr. Whittaker nodded again. "That's right," he said.

Patrick was excited. "How do we go after him?" he asked.

Mr. Whittaker turned to

the cousins. "The same way you did before. I'll send you to the time and place. You need to put on the ring and grab Hugh. Then all three of you will return to his time in 1450."

"Why can't you come with us?" Beth asked. "We have the ring now. Isn't that what stopped you before?"

Mr. Whittaker shook his head. "The Imagination Station program is confused. The machine still thinks that Hugh is *me*. So it won't let me in."

"For a really smart machine, it's kind of dumb," Patrick said.

Mr. Whittaker laughed. "The Imagination Station is a computer," he said. "And all computers have glitches in them."

Beth was worried. "How can we catch

Hugh?" she asked. "He doesn't trust us. He won't let us near him."

Mr. Whittaker knelt down in front of Beth. He looked in her eyes.

"You're going to have to outsmart him," Mr. Whittaker said. "You did it last time."

Patrick lifted his head. He was ready for the challenge. "We'll do it," he said.

Patrick's courage made Beth feel better. "We're ready," she said, smiling.

Mr. Whittaker stood and smiled at the cousins. He went back to the Imagination Station's keyboard.

"I'll send you to the exact place where Hugh landed," Mr. Whittaker said. "You'll arrive only a minute after he did."

Patrick checked his right-hand pants pocket. The ring was there. "Let's go!"

Patrick said. He stepped toward the Imagination Station.

"Wait a minute," Mr. Whittaker said. "You can't go in those clothes. You're still dressed in Old Testament tunics."

Mr. Whittaker waved his hand toward the two changing rooms. "You'll find new clothes in there."

The cousins knew the way it worked.

Patrick changed in the boys' changing room. When he came out, he frowned at Mr. Whittaker.

"These brown pants are too short," Patrick said. "They stop at my knees. And this collar looks like my grandma's!"

Beth came out of the girls' changing room. She was happier than Patrick was. She liked her skirt, apron, and red cape.

"Wait a minute," Beth said. "I've seen pictures of the Pilgrims. These clothes don't look right. The men wore hats with buckles, and all the clothes were black!"

Mr. Whittaker chuckled. "Those pictures aren't correct," he said. "The Pilgrims wore black only on days of worship. And there were no buckles on their hats."

Mr. Whittaker opened the door to the Imagination Station.

"Oh, I almost forgot," Mr. Whittaker said. He turned and went to the workbench. He picked up two items. "Your gifts."

He handed a golden hand mirror to Beth. A carving of an eagle was on the back.

"This is beautiful," Beth said. She looked at herself in the mirror. She giggled at her reflection.

Mr. Whittaker handed Patrick a brown leather pouch. A long drawstring held it shut.

"What's in here?" Patrick asked.

Mr. Whittaker smiled. "You'll see when the time comes."

Beth put the mirror in her apron pocket. Patrick put the pouch around his neck and under his shirt. They took their places in the Imagination Station seats. Mr. Whittaker closed the door. It made a loud *whoosh*!

Beth nodded to Patrick. Patrick pushed the red button.

The Imagination Station started to shake. Beth had gotten used to it by now. She wasn't scared anymore. But she wondered what might happen.

The machine whirred and rumbled. It seemed to move forward.

Then the rumbling grew louder.

Suddenly everything went black.

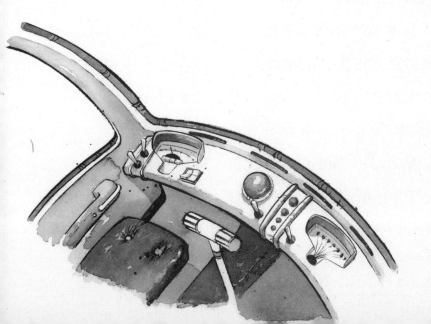

The Ambush

The darkness faded to light. The Imagination Station disappeared around Patrick and Beth.

The cousins sat on a large rock in the middle of thick woods.

"Cool!" Patrick said. "Is this Plymouth Rock?"

"What?" Beth asked.

"Plymouth Rock," Patrick said. "Isn't that where the Pilgrims landed?"

Beth shook her head. "I don't think
Plymouth Rock is in the middle of the woods.
How could they park the *Mayflower* here?"

There was a loud *snap* off to the left.
Patrick and Beth turned.

Patrick pointed and whispered. "It's Hugh."

Beth gasped.

Patrick raised his fingers to his lips. *Shhh!*

The cousins crept toward Hugh.

They ducked behind trees. They tiptoed as
they came closer. The woods opened into a
clearing.

Hugh's back was turned to them. He
seemed to be sitting on the edge of a cliff.

Now is our chance! Beth thought.

Patrick signaled to Beth that they should
come at him from both sides. Patrick got
into position.

They crept closer . . . closer . . .

Suddenly Hugh leaped to his feet. He spun around. "Stop!" he shouted.

Beth and Patrick stopped in their tracks.

Hugh's fists were in the air as if he expected a fight. Then he saw that it was the cousins. He frowned and dropped his hands.

"You again!" he said. "What are you doing here?"

Patrick said, "We came to take you home."

Hugh scowled. "Why would I want to go home? They'll arrest me as a thief. They'll throw me in Darkthorn's tower."

"But you don't belong here," Beth said.

Hugh shrugged. "This is better than a prison in England."

Beth wasn't sure what to do.

"Do you know where we are?" Hugh asked.

Patrick glanced at Beth. She saw his hand go to the pocket where he kept the ring.

"I can show you," Patrick said. He took a few steps toward Hugh. "But I'll have to draw a map in the dirt."

Hugh fixed his eyes on Patrick. "You have the ring, don't you?" he said. "I don't trust you."

Patrick moved slowly toward him. "We're trying to do what's right," he said.

Hugh smiled. "What you think is right and what I think is right are two different things."

Patrick took another step. "Come on," he said.

"Stay back!" Hugh shouted. Suddenly his eyes grew wide. He gasped loudly and raised his hands in fear. Then he jumped over the side of the cliff.

Beth screamed. She rushed to the edge and looked down.

It wasn't a cliff after all. There was a steep drop and then a dirt slope. Hugh half fell and half slid down the slope. He landed at

the
bottom
and ran away.
"Why did Hugh
look afraid?" Beth
asked.

19

"He saw something," Patrick said from beside her.

Then they realized they should look behind them.

The cousins turned and saw what had scared Hugh away.

Six Native American men stood there. They had bows loaded with arrows.

The warriors came straight at the cousins.

The Boy Pilgrim

Beth and Patrick raised their hands.

"We give up!" Patrick said. "Don't shoot!"

The Native Americans came closer. They kept their weapons raised.

Beth said, "Please! We're just kids!"

"I don't think they understand English," Patrick said. "Don't make any sudden moves."

The warriors surrounded Patrick and Beth. They still pointed their bows and arrows at the children.

One of the men shouted something in another language. Two of the men lowered their weapons. They grabbed the cousins.

"You're hurting my arm," Beth said.

"Don't complain," Patrick said. "Just stay quiet and follow along."

The Native Americans walked Patrick and Beth through the woods. They walked a long way. Then they came to a small village.

Patrick recognized the teepees from his history books. The homes were like brown upside-down ice-cream cones. The sides were made of animal skins.

The teepees circled a fire pit made from stones.

The two men led the cousins to one of

the teepees. One man lifted the tent flap. The other shoved them inside. It was dark and warm.

Patrick tried to adjust his eyes.

From the darkness a voice asked, "Who are you?"

Beth shrieked. Patrick jumped. He turned and saw a teenage boy.

The boy was sitting at the far side of the teepee. A small beam of light shone on his face. The light came from a hole in the roof.

"You spoke English!" Beth said.

"Of course I speak English," the boy said. "I'm not one of *them*."

"Who are you?" Patrick asked.

The boy leaned forward and said, "I'm John Billington Junior. Who are *you*?"

The cousins introduced themselves.

"Are you a Pilgrim?" Patrick asked.

"I'm a *prisoner*," John said.

"Why are those men holding you?" Beth asked.

"I was lost for five days," John said. "They found me and brought me here."

"You look sick," Beth said.

John said, "All I've had to eat are berries and nuts."

"That must be why you look so pale," Beth said.

"Pale?" John said.

Beth pulled the golden mirror out of her pocket. She handed it to the boy. "See?" she said.

John looked at the mirror. "Where did you get this?" he asked.

"A friend gave it to me," she said.

"Don't let the Indians see it if you want to keep it," John said. "They love trinkets like this. Indians are funny that way."

"*Native Americans*," Patrick said to correct him.

John frowned at Patrick. "Native what?"

"That's what we call the Indians at school," Beth said.

John shook his head. "Indians, savages," he said. "I don't care what you call them."

John looked at his face in the mirror. Then he stuck out his tongue. "I look all right," he said.

John handed the mirror back to Beth.

"Put this away before they steal it," he said.

"*Steal it*?" Patrick said. "Why are you talking about them like that? It's mean."

John shrugged. "We don't trust them. And they don't trust us," he said. "It's rather simple."

The flap to the teepee opened. A native man entered. He waved for the children to follow him.

John patted his chest as if to ask, "Do you want me too?"

The native waved again.

Patrick and Beth stepped into the daylight. Another native came over to the three captives. Together, the two men led them through the woods.

"I pray they're leading us back to my

village," John said.

"You mean . . . Plymouth?" Beth asked with excitement.

"Yes," John said.

Patrick had a million questions for John. "How long have you been in Plymouth?"

"We landed almost a year ago," he said. He slowly shook his head. "It has been very hard on us. The traders did us a lot of harm."

"The traders?" Patrick asked.

"They came from all over Europe to find gold," John said. "They stole what the Indians wouldn't trade. Many of the Indians were killed."

"They were killed for *gold*?" Beth asked, as if the idea were crazy.

"The Indians also died of a terrible

sickness," John added. "The traders brought the sickness with them from Europe."

"Whole villages—hundreds of people— were wiped out," Patrick said softly. He remembered learning about it in school.

Patrick heard one of the Native Americans speak angrily to the other. They began to argue.

Patrick wondered if the men were arguing about what to do with them.

"Why are *you* here?" Patrick asked. "Didn't you come for gold?"

"No," John said. "We came to farm the land and to trade in peace. But the Indians don't understand that. They think we're like the others. The Indians don't trust *anyone* with white skin."

The Native American man mumbled something and pointed. The children followed him.

John looked around and said, "This isn't the way back to Plymouth."

"Then where are they taking us?" Patrick asked.

"I don't know," John said.

They walked on. Beth asked, "Do you think they'll hurt us?"

"They won't hurt us unless they want to start a war," John said.

"It sounds like you're at war now," Patrick said.

"No. We're friends with some of the tribes," John said. "There's an Indian named Squanto who has helped us. He speaks English."

"Squanto?" Beth said. "I know him! He taught you how to plant corn. And how to use fish as fertilizer!"

John looked surprised. "How do you know that?"

Beth realized she had said too much.

"Are you from some other colony we don't know about?" John asked. "Who are you? How did you get here?"

Beth didn't know what to say.

Patrick cleared his throat. "We're from another part of the country," he said. "We've heard stories about Squanto."

John looked at them suspiciously. "What kinds of stories?" he asked.

Patrick thought for a moment. "He helped create a treaty between you and the Indians."

"That's true," John said. "We won't attack them. They won't attack us. We also made a promise. We'll help each other if enemy tribes or traders attack."

"But that's a good treaty!" Beth said. "So why don't you trust each other?"

"Because we're afraid," John said.

Patrick breathed in a salty ocean smell. He looked ahead. They were coming to another village. It was next to an ocean bay. The village was large and had many more teepees.

The native man took the children to the middle of the village. A large, dark-skinned man walked over to them. He wore a huge headdress of feathers.

This is the chief, Patrick thought.

The chief nodded to the native man

who had brought them. The man bowed and left.

The chief looked at each of the children and spoke. "I am Aspinet," he said. "Chief of the Nauset tribe."

He fixed his dark eyes on them. "You and your people have caused us much pain."

Patrick gulped and wondered, *Is the chief planning to cause* us *much pain in return?*

The Chief

Aspinet studied the cousins for a moment. Then his eaglelike eyes fixed on John.

"My warriors tell me that you and your friends are spies," Aspinet said.

"Spies! No!" John cried out. "I was lost. I couldn't find my village."

"You should not have left your village," Aspinet said. "We do not want you in our forests. Or anywhere near us."

"But—" John started.

"Your people make slaves of our people," Aspinet said with a scowl.

"Those weren't *my* people," John said. "*My* people—the ones in Plymouth, I mean—aren't here for slaves or for gold. We want to be your friends."

"Yet you stole from us," Aspinet said. "Friends do not steal from friends."

John shook his head. "We wouldn't steal from you."

"No? We buried corn for the winter. You stole it," Aspinet said.

John lowered his eyes. He looked guilty.

Beth guessed that the chief was telling the truth.

"Take them away," the chief said.

Two natives came forward.

"Please," John said. "Let me explain."

Aspinet turned his head and waved a hand to dismiss them.

The three children were led away by the Native Americans. They were put inside a teepee. Beth thought the animal-skin walls smelled like a burned steak.

The natives left. One stood guard just outside the tent.

John sat down and sighed.

Patrick stood over him. "Did someone from Plymouth steal the chief's corn?" he asked.

John nodded slowly. "Yes," he said. "Though we didn't mean to steal it."

"How could you steal something and not mean to?" Beth asked.

"We arrived in the winter," John said. "The voyage from England took longer than we thought. Sixty-seven days! Our food and supplies were almost gone. Many of our people died on the way."

Beth could imagine how hard it must have been. Two months on a ship is a long time.

John said, "When we landed here, we thought we would find food. But there wasn't much around."

John looked up at Beth. He had dark circles under his eyes. They were black against his pale skin. Beth noticed how thin he looked.

"More people died from starvation and sickness," John said. "Then one day we found a strange pile of branches. At first we thought it was a grave. Or maybe a store of weapons. So we dug it up. It was corn."

"The Indians stored the corn in the

ground?" Beth asked.

"That's how they store things," John said.

"That doesn't mean you're allowed to steal it," Patrick said.

"Our leaders thought the corn was a gift from God," John said. "We used the corn kernels for seeds."

Patrick folded his arms and frowned.

"We were going to replace the seed corn," said John.

"But you haven't yet," Beth said. Now she understood why Aspinet didn't trust the Pilgrims.

The opening to the teepee was pushed aside. A tall native man stepped inside with a basket. He dropped it on the ground and left again.

The basket was filled with bits of meat.

John leaped at the meat. He began to eat quickly.

Patrick and Beth hesitated.

"What is that?" Patrick asked.

John didn't look up. "I don't know," he said with a full mouth. "Deer. Perhaps beaver."

Suddenly there was a shout outside. More shouts followed. The camp stirred with activity.

Beth and Patrick peeked outside. Native American men were running to the shore. They carried bows, arrows, and spears.

The guard outside the teepee stayed where he was. He grunted a warning at the cousins.

Beth and Patrick watched as a small boat came into view. Its white sails fluttered in

the wind. There were ten men standing in the boat. All but one held muskets. They were dressed like Englishmen.

"Are they from Plymouth?" Beth asked.

John joined them at the teepee opening. "That's our shallop!" he shouted. "I see my father!"

The warriors raced toward the boat. They carried weapons.

Beth gasped. "The Pilgrims are going to be attacked!" she said.

The Shallop

The shallop came closer to the shore. The native warriors gathered. The men from Plymouth held up their muskets.

A tall, bearded man stood in the front of the boat. He was the only man without a gun. He held his hand up to the natives.

Patrick whispered to John, "Who's in the front?"

"That's William Bradford," John said.

"He's the new governor of Plymouth."

The shallop reached the shore. The natives didn't attack. But they kept their bows and arrows ready.

Some of the Englishmen pointed their muskets at the natives. Then two men jumped into the water. They pulled the boat onto the sand.

The Native Americans came forward. They raised their weapons as if they were going to attack.

The Englishmen leaped from the boat. They kept their muskets up and ready.

The two groups faced each other for a moment. The cousins held their breath.

Governor Bradford stepped toward the natives. He raised his hand. Then he lowered it.

"I think he's giving them the sign of peace," John said.

Governor Bradford turned to his men. He said something the children couldn't hear. The men lowered their guns to their sides.

Chief Aspinet strode across the sand. The large headdress made him appear very tall.

A group of Native American men came with him. They also carried weapons.

It looked as if there were a hundred natives. *If the Pilgrims and the natives fight, the natives will win*, Patrick thought.

The chief signaled his men. The ones with weapons stepped back. The ones without weapons followed the chief to the group of Englishmen.

Patrick asked, "Which one is your dad?"

John said, "The one in gray."

The man in gray stood off to one side. He turned his head quickly to the left and right.

"He's searching for you," Beth told John.

John nodded. He leaned out of the teepee and waved so his father could see him.

The guard slapped John's hand down. Then the man moved in front of the children. Now he blocked the opening. The children had to change positions to see the beach.

Governor Bradford and Chief Aspinet stood face-to-face. Governor Bradford bowed to Aspinet, and the chief bowed back.

Governor Bradford motioned to some men. They brought forward a small open box.

Aspinet reached inside. He lifted what looked like strands of beads.

"What are they doing?" Patrick whispered.

"Bradford is trading with them," John said.

The chief shook his head. He dropped the beads back into the box.

"He doesn't want them," said John.

Aspinet motioned to one of his warriors. Suddenly the warrior sprinted away. He ran toward their teepee. He spoke to the children's guard.

The guard grunted for the children to come out.

The warrior stepped in front of them. He had red paint streaked across his face. John moved as if he might run to his father. But the warrior put a heavy hand on his shoulder.

Aspinet called out. The warrior and guard moved aside.

Now the Englishmen could see the children. The men shouted with joy.

"John! John Junior!" Mr. Billington called out.

"God be praised," another man said.

Chief Aspinet motioned for them to come closer.

John, Patrick, and Beth followed the warrior.

They came within a few yards of the group. Then the chief held up his hand.

The warrior stopped. He held up his arms to keep the children back.

"Why won't they let us go?" Beth asked.

John looked worried. He said, "I think the chief plans to trade *us.*"

The Trade

Beth had a clearer view of the Englishmen. She thought Governor Bradford looked kind. She liked his thin face and scruffy beard.

The governor looked at her and then at Patrick. He seemed puzzled. Beth realized that the governor must be wondering who they were.

Chief Aspinet cleared his throat. "Speak," said the chief.

"My good friend," Governor Bradford said

with a bow. "We want to keep peace with all the Indian tribes. We have made a treaty with Chief Yellow Feather. We have agreed that no Indian will hurt an innocent man, woman, or child. So we have come to get our boy."

The chief grunted. "Chief Yellow Feather is not the chief of all our tribes."

"I know," Governor Bradford said. "But he is powerful, and your people respect him."

"Yellow Feather didn't ask me before he made the treaty with you," Aspinet said. "Why should I honor his treaty?"

"Because you desire peace among our peoples. Just as I do," Governor Bradford said.

Aspinet pointed to the box of beads. "Did you give Yellow Feather more than beads?"

The governor didn't answer.

Aspinet looked at the children. "Our peace and those children are worth more than beads," the chief said.

"You were right," Patrick whispered to John. "He's using us to trade."

Governor Bradford looked at the children and then nodded. He reached into his coat. He took out a knife in a leather case. He handed it to Aspinet. "This came from my country," Governor Bradford said. "You have nothing like it here."

Aspinet's eyes flickered with interest.

Beth remembered that Native Americans made knives out of sharp rocks. A steel knife from England would be very valuable to the chief.

Aspinet took the knife. He uncovered the

blade and studied it carefully. He ran a finger along the knife's sharp edge.

The chief grunted. He put the knife back in its case. "This is a fair trade for the boy," he said. He lifted his hand.

The warrior moved aside. The three children moved to go to Bradford, but the warrior grabbed Patrick and Beth. He shook his head at them.

John rushed to his father. Mr. Billington grabbed his son in a bear hug. He lifted him off the ground.

Aspinet asked, "What will you give in exchange for the second boy?"

Governor Bradford looked at Patrick. He didn't know who Patrick was. Beth was suddenly afraid the governor wouldn't trade anything for Patrick. Or for her.

Governor Bradford turned to Aspinet. "I have another knife. It's mine." He reached inside his coat again. This time the exchange was quick. Aspinet didn't inspect the weapon.

"What about the girl?" Aspinet said.

Governor Bradford looked at Beth. She looked back. Her eyes pleaded with him.

The governor looked at her helplessly. He said to Aspinet, "The beads are all I have left."

"Not good enough," the chief said.

Suddenly Beth had an idea.

"I have something!" she called out.

All eyes turned to her.

Patrick looked at her. "What are you doing?"

Beth reached in her pocket. She pulled

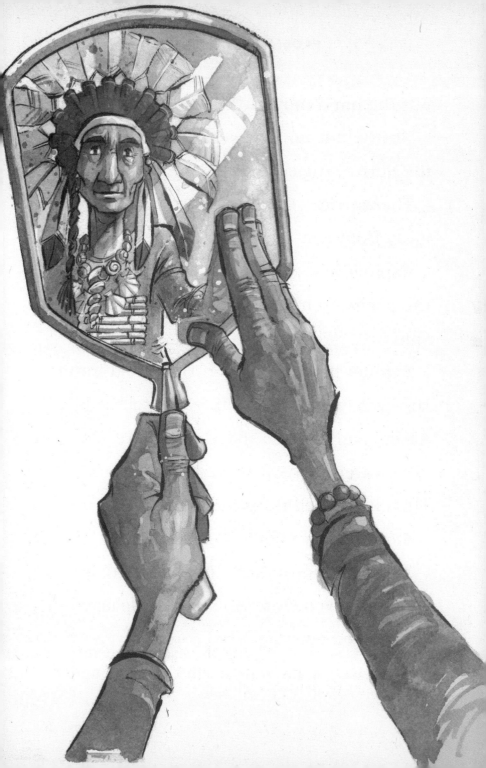

out the hand mirror. "I have this," she said.

She held it up. The sun's rays bounced off the mirror. It gleamed.

The warrior seemed startled and stepped away from her.

Aspinet held out his hand. Beth carried the mirror to him. "It's called a mirror," she said.

Aspinet took the mirror. He looked into it. His eyes grew large. Beth could tell he had never seen his face so clearly before. The chief carefully turned the mirror around. Then he turned it upside down.

Governor Bradford smiled at Beth.

Aspinet held up the mirror. The other natives moved closer to see. They gasped and moved away.

Beth saw a smile form on the chief's face.

He nodded at Beth. "You may go," he said.

Beth joined Patrick and John.

The governor ordered everyone to get into the shallop.

As the Englishmen moved, Aspinet shouted, "Wait! We're not finished!"

Governor Bradford waited.

"You have stolen corn from us," the chief said.

Governor Bradford bowed slightly. "Yes, great chief. We've wronged you, but we will make it right."

"How?" asked the chief.

"Send some of your men to our colony. Then we'll gladly give back what we took," said the governor. "I'm sorry."

Chief Aspinet seemed to think for a moment. "I will send my men," he finally said with a nod.

Next the Englishmen helped the cousins into the shallop. Then the governor climbed aboard. The rest of the men joined them.

Beth noticed that the Englishmen never took their eyes off the warriors. Just in case.

But the natives weren't interested in the Pilgrims. Instead they gathered around Aspinet to look at the mirror.

The shallop moved away from the shore. Governor Bradford sat down next to the cousins. "Who are you? How did you get here?" he asked.

Patrick and Beth looked at each other. Beth thought they should know what to say by now. But it was always awkward to explain.

Governor Bradford asked, "Are you the

children of traders or those seeking freedom to worship? Do you live far from here?"

"Very far," Patrick said.

"It must be," the governor said. He sounded confused. "I know of no settlements near here."

"We came to find a man who is lost," Beth said.

"Has he been captured by the Indians?" Governor Bradford asked.

"We don't know," Patrick said. "He ran off into the woods."

The governor frowned. "It's not safe for a white man to wander around alone," he said.

Just then John and Mr. Billington came over.

"Thank you for saving my son," Mr. Billington said to Governor Bradford.

"I'm truly grateful, sir," added John.

"You shouldn't thank me," said Governor Bradford. "Chief Yellow Feather told us where you were. You owe him your life."

After an hour, the shallop approached the shore. Beth heard a shout.

A man was running down the beach.

"Hurry, governor!" he shouted. "Something terrible has happened!"

The governor stood. "What is it? What's wrong?" he called to the man.

"An attack!" the man cried out. "There's been an attack!"

Kidnapped!

The shallop landed. Beth, Patrick, and the Pilgrims scrambled to shore.

Governor Bradford rushed to the shouting man. "Calm down," he said. "Tell me what happened."

The man was almost breathless. He said between gasps, "Chief . . . Yellow Feather's . . . village has been . . . attacked."

"By whom?" Governor Bradford asked.

"Chief Corbitant and . . . his tribe," the

man said. He took a deep breath. Then he blurted, "Corbitant wants to break the power of Chief Yellow Feather."

Governor Bradford sighed. "It didn't take long for the treaty to be tested," he said.

"It's worse," said the man. "They've kidnapped Squanto!"

The governor's eyes widened. "Call the men to the meeting hall," he said.

The man rushed off.

The cousins walked with the governor and the other men. They approached the Plymouth plantation.

Patrick was surprised at how bare the place was. There was a makeshift fence around simple wooden-frame houses. The roofs were made of thatch. Each house looked as if it had a giant bird's nest on top.

"You're not members of our colony. And so you'll have to wait outside," Governor Bradford said. He went with a group of men into a two-story building.

"There seems to be a lot of trouble around here," Beth said to Patrick.

"I wonder if Hugh has anything to do with it?" said Patrick.

Patrick paced back and forth outside the meetinghouse. Beth drifted over to the door.

"Patrick," she whispered. "I can hear what they're saying."

Patrick joined her at the door.

The men were arguing. One was concerned about Squanto. What would they do if he had been killed? Another man asked why they should help Chief Yellow Feather. "These are Indians fighting against Indians," he said. "It's none of our business."

Governor Bradford said, "It *is* our business! We signed a treaty with Chief Yellow Feather. He helped us find young John Billington. We promised that we would protect each other. We promised that we would fight for each other."

"Treaties are often broken," said another man.

"Perhaps so," said Governor Bradford. "But not by us. As Christians we will act with honesty and loyalty."

Another man said, "It's foolish to put ourselves in danger. Do you want to die protecting savages? There are fewer than twenty men here."

The governor spoke loudly and clearly. "Chief Yellow Feather and Squanto are our friends. We wouldn't have survived without their help."

A man with a deep voice shouted, "Confound it! Our action must be swift and sure. We must show that our people—and the friends of our people—are not to be wronged."

"Captain Standish is right," proclaimed the governor. "We'll rescue Squanto, or we'll die trying."

The Doctor

Governor Bradford made an announcement. Captain Myles Standish would take ten men to rescue Squanto the next morning. None of the Pilgrim children would be allowed to go.

That night the cousins stayed with the Billingtons. Mrs. Billington let Beth sleep on a straw mattress. Patrick had to sleep on the floor.

Beth fell asleep listening to Mr. Billington

grumble. He said that he didn't like Captain Standish. He also didn't like the treaty with the "savages." He didn't trust them.

The next thing Beth knew, someone was shaking her shoulder. She opened her eyes. Patrick was staring down at her.

"What's wrong?" she asked quietly.

"We're going to follow the rescue team," Patrick whispered.

Beth sat up. "But we're not allowed to go," she said.

"The Pilgrim children aren't allowed," said Patrick. "We're not Pilgrims."

"It will be dangerous," Beth said.

"We have to take that chance," Patrick said. "I think Hugh has something to do with this."

Beth agreed. She got up. She and Patrick

sneaked out of the Billingtons' house.

The Plymouth men had gathered. They stood at the edge of the woods.

"We have to stay back so nobody sees us," Patrick said. They made their way through the plantation. They hid around the side of a small shack.

Suddenly a voice said from behind them, "Did I hear you say you're going along?"

Beth stifled a scream. Patrick spun around. It was John Billington Junior.

"What are you doing here?" Patrick whispered.

"I'm going with you," said John.

"Governor Bradford said you can't," Beth said.

John shrugged as if he didn't care what Governor Bradford said. "Besides," he said.

"I know this area better than you do."

"Oh, really?" Beth said. "Then how did you get lost?"

John ignored her. "We want to stay close to *him*." He pointed to a short man with red hair.

"Who's that?" Patrick asked.

"That's Captain Myles Standish. He's in charge of our military," John said. He leaned forward and grinned. "My brother and I sometimes call him Captain Shrimp!" He said it with a giggle.

Patrick saw the rescue party leaving. He moved to follow.

Beth and John did too.

But a man's voice said, "Oh no, you don't!"

Mr. Billington grabbed his son by the collar.

"But I want to go!" said John Junior.

"After all the trouble you caused us?" Mr. Billington asked. "You're not going anywhere."

Then Mr. Billington looked at the cousins. "You two," he said. "Come help with chores. No one gets to eat for free."

He dragged his son away. Patrick and Beth had no choice. They followed the Billingtons back to the house.

Late the next day, the search party returned. The Pilgrim men brought back three Native Americans: two warriors and one squaw.

Beth could tell that all three natives had been hurt. They walked slowly. Blood covered their clothes.

Beth wondered what had gone wrong. She

wanted to talk to Patrick, but he was out working in the fields with John Junior and his brother, Francis.

The Englishmen brought the natives to the meetinghouse.

Governor Bradford asked Beth to help the doctor. Now Beth was allowed inside the building. She learned that the natives had been shot by accident.

Beth thought Dr. Fuller looked older than most of the Pilgrim men. His head was bald on top. But he had bushy white hair around the sides of his head.

Beth went into the meeting room. The wounded Native Americans lay on straw mattresses. Beth and two Pilgrim women helped Dr. Fuller. They placed damp cloths on the foreheads of the patients.

Dr. Fuller opened a wooden chest. He took out some herbs and a small knife. Then he mixed a paste with herbs, hot water, and bread. He spread the paste on cloths. He placed the cloths on the wounds.

The Native Americans slept.

Beth waited and prayed silently. She

asked God to heal the Native Americans.

"The wounds don't look too bad," Dr. Fuller said. "All three Indians should be fine."

About three hours passed. The patients woke. They sat up and looked at Dr. Fuller. They made motions with their arms.

"It looks like they want to go home," Beth said.

The natives got up. Then they walked out of the meetinghouse.

Dr. Fuller and Beth followed them. "Don't leave," he said to the natives.

"We'll take care of you," Beth called out.

The Native Americans didn't seem to hear them. The men and the squaw slowly walked away.

Beth felt sad. A few minutes later, Captain

Standish and Governor Bradford came to the meetinghouse.

"I saw the Indians leaving," Captain Standish said.

"We did all we could," said Dr. Fuller.

"You're a good man, Dr. Fuller," Governor Bradford said. "I'm sure they are leaving as our friends."

"More likely not. We shot them," Captain Standish said. He shook his head.

"What happened in the village?" Dr. Fuller asked.

"The men and I waited until dark at the Indian village," Captain Standish said. "Then we moved in. We wanted to search for Squanto peacefully. But something went wrong. I thought I heard someone shout 'fire.'"

"Who was it?" Governor Bradford asked.

"I didn't recognize the voice," Captain Standish said. "I think it came from a stranger."

"Another hostage?" Dr. Fuller asked.

"I don't know," said the captain.

Beth caught her breath. *Could it have been Hugh?* she wondered.

"Then the Indians screamed," Captain Standish said. "We fired our muskets." He paused and looked at the floor.

"What about Squanto?" Dr. Fuller asked.

"He wasn't there. It was all a mistake. Squanto wasn't kidnapped. Someone made up the story to cause trouble," said Captain Standish.

Hugh, Beth thought.

"That's too bad," Dr. Fuller said. "Will the

tribe seek revenge?"

"Let's hope they see that we are men of action. They'd be wise not to attack us," the captain said.

"What if you're wrong?" Governor Bradford asked. "What if they decide to join together against us?"

Captain Standish said, "Then we need to prepare for an attack!"

The Missing Musket

All the men of Plymouth Colony were called in from the fields.

Patrick came with them. He complained about his aching muscles.

Beth told him about the wounded Native Americans. She also told him about the voice Captain Standish had heard.

The cousins decided to go back to the meetinghouse. It was the center of the plantation's military strength. It also had a second floor where they could see everything that happened.

On that floor, a large cannon sat next to two very small ones. Cannonballs were stacked nearby. Some of the balls were the size of oranges. Others were the size of large beans.

Beth peeked out of a hole in the wall. A cannon barrel was meant to fit in the hole.

"The men are marching," she said.

Patrick looked through another hole. Governor Bradford marched with the men.

Then Captain Standish ordered them to load their weapons.

The men obeyed. Patrick watched a man take a small pouch of gunpowder from his belt. He poured the gunpowder into a long musket barrel. He dropped a musket ball down the barrel. Then he picked up a long stick. He packed down the powder and the ball.

To shoot, the man had to light a rope fuse. That would set the gunpowder on fire.

"Fire when ready!" the captain shouted.

The men dropped to one knee and fired at targets in a nearby field.

Blam!

"That's a lot of work," Patrick said.

"How can they fire more than one shot in a battle?" Beth asked.

"Bows and arrows are faster," Patrick said.

Beth looked up, thoughtful. "What is Hugh up to?"

Patrick paced around. "Do you think Hugh wants to be a chief?"

Beth shook her head. "They wouldn't trust

a white man to be their chief," Beth said. "Maybe he's causing trouble to draw us out."

Patrick nodded. "Hugh wants the ring. So he'll come here to get it."

"Which means he's sneaking around here somewhere," Beth said with a shiver. "I don't like that."

There was a commotion down below. Patrick and Beth leaned through the cannon holes.

"Calm down and speak plainly, boy," Captain Standish was saying to John Billington Junior.

"Someone has stolen my musket, sir."

"Stolen? That seems unlikely," Captain Standish said. "Where did you last see it?"

"Outside my house. I leaned it against the wall. I went back inside to get my powder horn," John said.

"When was this?" Captain Standish asked.

Mr. Billington stepped forward. "It happened around the time the wounded Indians left us," he said.

"Do you believe *they* stole the gun?" Governor Bradford asked him.

"They must have," said Mr. Billington.

Captain Standish shook his head. "I watched the Indians leave. They carried no weapons."

"Well, *someone* took my son's musket!" Mr. Billington said.

Patrick and Beth looked at each other.

"Hugh," the cousins said.

Patrick and Beth raced down to the ground floor. They caught up to John Junior at his house.

"John," Patrick said, "think back to when your gun was taken. Did you see a stranger?"

"I know everyone here," he said. "I saw no strangers."

"Did anything strange happen when your gun was taken?" Beth asked.

John thought for a moment. "I thought my brother Francis was playing a prank on me."

"What kind of prank?" Patrick asked.

"Hiding around the corner and spying on me. I was burying the gunpowder barrel under the storeroom," John said. "I thought I saw him out of the corner of my eye."

"Why was the gunpowder barrel buried under the storeroom?" Patrick asked.

"So our enemies won't find it," John said.

John lifted the cow's horn that was

around his neck. It hung from a leather strap. "My father sent me to get the gunpowder for our horns," he said.

"Then what happened?" Beth asked.

"I brought the gunpowder back here to fill our horns," John said. "I stepped outside with my gun. But I forgot my horn. So I went back inside to fetch it."

"What happened after that?" Beth asked.

"When I came outside again, my musket was gone," John said. "At first I thought my brother had taken it. But it couldn't have been him. He was over in the field with my father."

Patrick looked at Beth. *It had to be Hugh.*

"How am I going to fight the Indians now?" John said. He frowned. He picked up a thin sword. It was slightly bent and rusty. "This will have to do," he said and walked off.

Beth and Patrick walked back in the same direction. They headed toward the marching men.

"What can Hugh do with one musket?" Beth asked. "Will he shoot us to get the ring?"

Patrick said, "What if Hugh used the Imagination Station to take a musket back to his time? In 1450 they didn't have guns like that. He'd be the most powerful person back then. It would change history."

"Can we really change history in the Imagination Station?" Beth asked.

"I think we're changing it by being here," Patrick said. "But I don't know if it *stays* changed. We can't take any chances."

The cousins picked up their pace.

They reached the men. Everyone looked nervous. Some looked afraid.

"What's wrong?" Patrick asked John Junior.

"A scout just came in," John replied. "A large army of Indians is coming."

The Treaty

Captain Standish was small, but his voice was not. "We will make our stand at the edge of the woods," he shouted to the Pilgrims. "We can hold the Indians off there."

The cousins watched everyone scramble around. Some took fighting positions. Others ran for cover.

Patrick watched for Hugh. He might use a battle to get to them.

Captain Standish and his men gathered on the crest of a small hill. They formed two lines. One group of men knelt in front. The other group stood up behind them. All of the men had their muskets pointed toward the forest.

"Don't fire until I give the word," Captain Standish said.

For a few moments, it was very quiet. The only noise was the chirping of the birds.

Phhht!

A single arrow came out of nowhere. It stuck into a tree behind Captain Standish.

"First line fire when I say!" Captain Standish said. The men took aim.

"Wait!" a voice called out. It was

Governor William Bradford.

Captain Standish turned. "What is it, governor?"

Governor Bradford went to the arrow. "This arrow has a wrapping."

"A wrapping?" the captain asked.

The governor pulled the arrow from the tree. "There's a piece of leather wrapped around the shaft."

"Keep your eyes on that forest," Captain Standish said. He came over to Governor Bradford. The governor untied the leather. The cousins came closer.

Governor Bradford held up the leather wrap. Scratched into it was the word *peace*.

"Is it a trick?" Captain Standish asked.

"What Indian knows how to *write* in

English?" Governor Bradford asked.

"There is only one," said Captain Standish. "Squanto!"

Patrick leaned toward Beth. "Or Hugh?"

Governor Bradford held the leather note like a flag. He walked toward the woods.

"Don't be a fool!" Mr. Billington shouted after him.

Governor Bradford called out. "Squanto!"

Patrick and Beth braced themselves. If this was a trick, the governor could be seriously hurt.

"Squanto! If you want peace, then come out!" the governor said.

One by one, Native American men rose up from the bushes. They came out from behind the trees.

One stepped out from the rest of them. He wore a white man's jacket. He approached Governor Bradford.

"My friend," the man said.

"Squanto!" Governor Bradford said.

Patrick
and Beth
sighed with relief.

Governor Bradford held Squanto's
arm. "I'm happy to see you alive."

Squanto pointed to three people

nearby. Patrick recognized them as the natives who had been wounded. "Thank you for healing them," Squanto said.

"We're sorry they were hurt," Governor Bradford said.

"You thought I was in danger," Squanto said. "You have honored the treaty."

Squanto bowed down in front of Governor Bradford. "We now wish to honor you," Squanto said.

The governor looked embarrassed. He touched Squanto's shoulder. "Stand up, my friend. Let us honor all of our people." He looked as if he had an idea. "A feast!" he said. "We shall host a feast. Will you and Chief Yellow Feather's tribe join us?"

"I'll ask Chief Yellow Feather," Squanto said. "I'm sure he will say yes."

Captain Standish told his men to stand down. With a smile he announced, "There will be no war today."

A few of the men clapped their hands. Everyone looked relieved.

"A feast?" Beth said to Patrick. "Could that be the first Thanksgiving?"

Patrick nodded. "It must be."

"But what about Hugh?" she asked.

"We have to stay close to everyone else," Patrick said. "Hugh wants the ring. He won't get that without us."

"A feast is the perfect way for him to sneak in," said Beth.

The cousins looked at one another nervously.

Thanksgiving

The Pilgrims prepared for the feast. The men brought out wooden planks. They laid the planks on sawhorses. These would be the tables.

There was so much food, the planks bent in the middle.

Nine Pilgrim women were there—four adults and five teenage girls. They cooked the meats and vegetables. Beth helped them. There were plates of wild onions, wild berries, carrots, cabbages, and pumpkins.

Chief Yellow Feather led his tribe. The natives came out of the woods and walked to the tables. The chief wore special beads. His headdress was colorful and tall.

Most of the natives brought their own food—deer, pheasant, and turkey. There were more Native Americans than anyone in Plymouth expected.

Patrick and Beth stayed near Captain Standish and Governor Bradford.

"We're vastly outnumbered," Captain Standish said to the governor.

Governor Bradford smiled and said, "Be at peace, Captain. If only for one day."

Beth looked at Patrick. He was also watching nervously.

"Captain," Patrick called out to Standish.

"Yes, lad?" the captain answered.

"Is someone guarding the storehouse?" Patrick asked.

Captain Standish nodded. "I wouldn't leave it unattended," he said. "Francis Billington is watching it." The captain walked off toward the tables.

"Why are you worried about that?" Beth asked Patrick.

"Hugh has a musket, but he needs powder. And he'll need flint and bullets," Patrick said. "He'll have to sneak those out of the storeroom. Then he'll come looking for us."

Beth looked around. There wasn't a sad face in the whole crowd. She was sorry that Hugh might spoil it.

Soon everyone was settled at the long tables or on the grass. Governor Bradford stood up and quieted the group down.

Governor Bradford asked everyone to bow their heads in prayer.

Squanto listened to what the governor said. Then he repeated the words to the natives in their own language.

Some of the natives prayed with the Pilgrims. Other natives looked confused.

"Our God in heaven," the governor prayed, "we thank You for a bountiful harvest. For food and friendships, we thank You. For this new land. For the chance to worship You freely as our Lord and our God. Bless us as we live together in service to You. Amen."

Beth helped serve Native Americans and Pilgrims at their tables. She placed food on their wooden plates.

Everyone shared one bowl for drinking.

It had four handles. Beth beamed as she moved around from table to table. She served men, women, and children. But she didn't feel like a servant. She felt as if she was a part of something special.

Later Beth sat down and ate. But she said, "No, thank you," when someone passed her the eel.

Patrick nibbled at his food, but he kept glancing toward the storehouse.

After the meal, every person had something fun to do. The Pilgrims held a military parade. The Native Americans danced. The children had running and jumping contests. The men moved to an empty field and held target practice. The native warriors shot their bows and arrows.

Then the Plymouth men stood up to shoot

their muskets.

The guns banged like big firecrackers. Beth winced each time they went off. *Blam! Blam! Blam!*

Patrick looked worried again. "If these men loaded their guns," he said, "then they had to dig up the powder kegs."

"So?" Beth asked.

"Did they bury them again?" Patrick asked.

"How am I supposed to know?" Beth said.

More men fired their muskets.

Patrick pointed. "That's the Billington family. *All* of them," he said.

"So?" Beth asked again.

"So who is watching the storehouse?" Patrick asked. He stood up.

Blam! Blam! Blam! the guns sounded.

And then: *Blam!*

Beth noticed something strange about the last shot. "Patrick," she said. "Did you hear that?"

"It was a gunshot," Patrick said. "But it came from the storehouse." He dashed away.

Beth groaned and chased after him.

Hugh Again

Patrick and Beth ran as fast as they could.

The pouch's strap tightened around Patrick's neck. He pulled it out of his shirt so he could breathe. The pouch thudded against his chest as he ran.

Beth's braids bounced as she sprinted.

The storehouse door stood open.

"Someone's in there," Patrick whispered.

Then the door opened wider. Hugh stood with a musket pointed at them. "This was easy. Come in," he said.

Patrick felt foolish. His mind raced with ways to escape.

The cousins stepped into the building.

"Farther in," Hugh said.

The cousins moved toward the middle of the building. Barrels were stacked to the ceiling. One had a hole in it. Some kind of liquid trickled out.

Baskets, bolts of cloth, powder horns, and animal skins were scattered about. The room had the smell of gunpowder.

"Give me the ring," Hugh said with a sneer.

Patrick looked at the pouch.

"Hand it over," Hugh said. He raised the musket so it was level with Patrick's chest.

Patrick lifted the leather strap over his head. The pouch felt heavy. *I wonder what's*

in it, Patrick thought. *I hope it's nothing
Hugh can use to hurt us.*

"Don't give it to him," Beth said.

Patrick nodded at the musket. "I have to,"
he said.

"Open it up," Hugh said.

Patrick fumbled with the lace around the
top of the pouch. It took a
minute, but he finally got
it open. He saw the
glint of gold. He tossed
the pouch to Hugh.

Hugh smiled greedily.

Beth frowned. "I hope you wind up in
dinosaur times. And then get chased by a
T. rex," she said.

"A what?" Hugh asked.

"Never mind," said Beth.

Hugh used one hand to hold the musket. He used the other hand to turn the pouch upside down. Out dropped a ring.

That's Albert's ring, Patrick thought. Then he got an idea on why Mr. Whittaker put it in the pouch.

"Ha!" Hugh said. His eyes were bright. He held the ring in one hand. A smile stretched across his face. He waved the musket.

"Imagine what a weapon like this will mean in my time," he said, "I will have more power than the king."

"A gun doesn't give you power," Beth said. "Real power comes from something you'll never understand."

Hugh didn't seem to be listening. He moved to another barrel and lifted the lid. He picked up a handful of musket balls.

"These will do."

He took the pouch and filled it with musket balls. The pouch bulged.

Beth looked at Patrick.

He was watching Hugh carefully.

Hugh took a few steps away from the cousins. He gathered the powder horn, the pouch, and the musket close to him. Then he held up the ring.

"Now for the magic chariot," Hugh said.

"We have to stop him," Beth whispered.

"Wait," said Patrick.

"Wait for what?" Beth asked.

"You chatter like a couple of squirrels," Hugh said. He held up the ring and slipped it on his finger.

The Cave

Hugh pushed the ring all the way onto his ring finger.

The Imagination Station appeared. Hugh jumped inside.

"No!" Beth shouted. She leaped at the machine. But it was too late.

There was a flash of light. The Imagination Station disappeared.

Beth looked at Patrick. Disappointment filled her eyes.

But Patrick was smiling. He reached into his pocket.

He held up Mr. Whittaker's ring. "Let's go to England in 1450," he said. "That's where Mr. Whittaker sent Hugh."

"But how?" Beth asked.

"Hugh put on *Albert's* ring," Patrick said. "And it took Hugh back to Albert's time."

Beth laughed and took hold of Patrick's arm.

In one quick move, Patrick slipped the ring on his finger.

There was a flash of light.

Suddenly, everything went black.

Beth heard the familiar *whoosh* of the door and the whir of the machine.

Then there was silence.

Beth didn't know why it was still
dark. She was sure they weren't in the
Imagination Station anymore.

She felt a jolt. The two of them tumbled
to the ground. It was as if the Imagination
Station had tossed them out.

She heard Hugh groan.

"Where am I?" Hugh asked.

Sir Andrew the knight and James the
squire came into view. They stood looking at
Hugh. They looked amazed.

Beth knew they were back in the cave. It
was the place where Hugh had grabbed the
ring and escaped into time.

Hugh jumped to his feet. "No!" he said.

Beth and Patrick stood.

Hugh searched around him. "Where is my

musket?" he asked.

Sir Andrew lifted a sword.

Hugh looked as if he might run for it.

"Stay where you are, coward!" Sir Andrew shouted. He came closer with the blade.

Hugh lifted up his hands in surrender. He sneered.

"To the castle," Sir Andrew said.

Hugh glared at Beth and Patrick with a nasty scowl. He moved slowly toward the mouth of the cave.

"Well done, Patrick and Beth," Sir Andrew said before they left the cave.

Patrick turned to James. "Will Hugh be put in Lord Darkthorn's tower?" he asked.

"Yes," James said. "Lord Darkthorn himself will deal with the villain."

"Were you waiting here all this time?"

Patrick asked James.

James looked puzzled. "You were gone only a few minutes. We had gone back to the secret room. Then we heard Hugh groan."

Patrick and Beth looked at each other. *Only a few minutes*, Beth thought.

Patrick looked down at the ring on his finger. It seemed to glow.

There was a hum behind them. The Imagination Station came into view.

"Time to go," Patrick said.

"It was nice meeting you," Beth said to James.

James bowed. "It was an honor."

The cousins climbed inside the Imagination Station.

Beth pushed the red button.

Whit's End

Patrick and Beth stepped out of the
Imagination Station. They were back in
the workshop at Whit's End.

Mr. Whittaker smiled at them.
"Welcome back!"

The cousins hugged him.

"Mission accomplished!" Beth said.

"Hugh is where he belongs," Patrick
said to Mr. Whittaker. "Here's your ring."

Mr. Whittaker took the ring. "Thank

you," he said. "I'll keep it safe."

The cousins went into the changing rooms. They put on their normal clothes.

"Tell me about your adventure," Mr. Whittaker said when they came back.

The cousins talked for an hour. They told Mr. Whittaker about everything that had happened.

When they finished, Mr. Whittaker said, "I hope you understand how hard it was for the Pilgrims. They went through a lot so they could worship freely as Christians."

Beth nodded. She said, "I think they learned a lot about getting along with the Native Americans too."

"The Pilgrims were honest and trustworthy," Mr. Whittaker said. "Those values come from the Bible."

Mr. Whittaker reached over and pushed a button on the side of the Imagination Station. The machine's hum faded away. The lights went dim and then turned off.

"That was quite an adventure," Mr. Whittaker said. "Thank you for all your help."

"That's it?" Patrick asked. "We can't have any more?"

"I thought you'd be tired after everything you've done," Mr. Whittaker said.

"Tired!" said Beth. "We're ready to go again."

Mr. Whittaker chuckled. "Come back tomorrow," he said. "And we'll see what we can come up with."

"See you tomorrow!" the cousins said, along with their goodbyes.

Patrick and Beth left Whit's End and walked in the summer sunlight. Each wondered what kind of adventure they would have next.

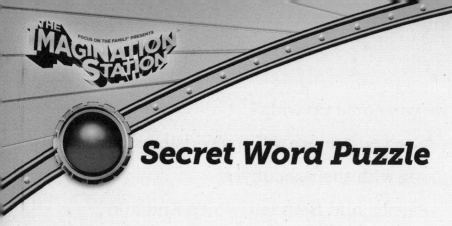
Secret Word Puzzle

Fill in the five clues. Then you'll know the secret word and what the Pilgrims wanted more than gold.

1 The colony that the cousins visited:

☐ __ __ __ __ __ __ __.

2 Indian Chief who came to the first Thanksgiving: Yellow

__ ☐ __ __ __ __ __.

3 The name of the Pilgrims' big ship:

__ ☐ __ __ __ __ __ __ __.

4 The food Squanto taught the Pilgrims to plant.

☐ __ __ __.

5 Hugh stole this from John Junior: A

__ __ __ __ ☐ __.

Each answer has a letter in a box. Write those letters, in order, in the boxes below. The answer is the secret word:

☐ ☐ ☐ ☐ ☐

AUTHOR MARIANNE HERING
is former editor of *Focus on the Family Clubhouse*® magazine. She has written more than a dozen children's books. She likes to take walks in the rain with her golden retriever, Chase.

ILLUSTRATOR DAVID HOHN draws and paints books, posters, and projects of all kinds. He works from his studio in Portland, Oregon.

AUTHOR MARSHAL YOUNGER has written over 100 Adventures in Odyssey® radio dramas and the children's book series Kidsboro. He lives in Tennessee with his wife and four children. He has been a Cleveland Indians fan for 34 long years.

FOCUS ON THE FAMILY®

No matter who you are, what you're going through, or what challenges your family may be facing, we're here to help. With practical resources —like our toll-free Family Help Line, counseling, and Web sites— we're committed to providing trustworthy, biblical guidance, and support.

Focus on the Family Clubhouse Jr.

Creative stories, fascinating articles, puzzles, craft ideas, and more are packed into each issue of *Focus on the Family Clubhouse Jr.*® magazine. You'll love the way this bright and colorful magazine reinforces biblical values and helps boys and girls (ages 3–7) explore their world. **Subscribe now at Clubhousejr.com.**

Focus on the Family Clubhouse

Through an appealing combination of encouraging content and entertaining activities, *Focus on the Family Clubhouse*® magazine (ages 8–12) will help your children—or kids you care about—develop a strong Christian foundation. **Subscribe now at Clubhousemagazine.com.**